This book belongs to

....

*For my son, Tim, who is deciding
what to do with the rest of his life.*

First published in Great Britain in 1998 by Andersen Press Ltd.,
20 Vauxhall Bridge Road, London SW1V 2SA. This paperback
edition first published in 2017 by Andersen Press Ltd.
Copyright © Colin McNaughton, 1998
The rights of Colin McNaughton to be identified as the author and illus-
trator of this work have been asserted by him in accordance with the
Copyright, Designs and Patents Act, 1988.
All rights reserved. Colour separated in Italy by Fotoriproduzioni
Beverari, Verona. Printed and bound in China.

10 9 8 7 6 5 4 3 2 1

British Library Cataloguing in Publication Data available.

ISBN 978 1 78344 555 4

No animals were hurt in the
making of this book. Oh, except
Mister Wolf, of course.

Colin McNaughton

Hmm...

A

Andersen Press

London

"Well, clever chops," said Mister Wolf. "What sort of job do you suggest?"
"Well," said Preston, "what do you want to be?"
"Hmm…" said Mister Wolf. "Full-up."
"What are you good at?" said Preston.

"Hmm…" said Mister Wolf.
"Eating pigs."
"And what do you enjoy?"
said Preston.
"Hmm…" said Mister Wolf.
"Eating pigs *and* being full-up."

"You could be a footballer," said Preston. "Hmm…" said Mister Wolf. "I wouldn't mind a shot at that."

"You could be a school teacher," said Preston. "Hmm…" said Mister Wolf. "I could certainly teach you a lesson or two!"

"You could be a pilot," said Preston. "Hmm…" said Mister Wolf. "That would suit me down to the ground."

"You could be a poet," said Preston. "Hmm…" said Mister Wolf. "I could do verse, I suppose."

"You could be a crane driver," said Preston. "Hmm..." said Mister Wolf. "That's a smashing idea!"

"You could be a sailor," said Preston. "Hmm…" said Mister Wolf. "I could take that idea on board."

"You could be a cook," said Preston. "Hmm…" said Mister Wolf. "A very tasty idea!"

"So Mister Wolf,"
said Preston,
"What do you think?"

"Hmm…" said Mister Wolf,
"It's certainly
food for thought!"

Suddenly!

Preston. Dinner's ready!

Coming mum!

Preston! Have you left that window open?

Sorry mum.

I'll close it.

Thanks dad.

Huh! It's alright for some! I have to find my _own_ dinner!

I mean, people don't realize what hard work it is catching pigs! All that scheming and creeping about— all that sneaking around... grumble.. .grumble...